Chickens

by Bobby Lynn Maslen
pictures by John R. Maslen

Scholastic Inc.
New York   Toronto   London   Auckland   Sydney

Also available:

Bob Books
for Beginning Readers

More Bob Books
For Young Readers

For more Bob Books ask for them at your local bookstore or call: 1-800-733-5572.

No part of this publication may be reproduced in whole or in part, or stored in a retrieval system, or transmitted in any form or by any means, electronic, mechanical, photocopying, recording, or otherwise, without written permission of the publisher. For information regarding permission, write to Bob Books™ Publications, Box 633, West Linn, OR 97068.

ISBN 0-590-22421-2

12 11 10 9 8 7 6 5 4 3 2   4 5 6 7 8 9/9

Printed in the U.S.A.   10

First Scholastic printing, October 1994

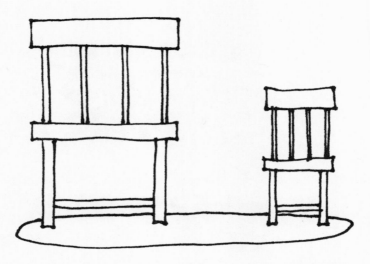

Chicken Big and Chicken Little had
two chairs, a big chair and a little chair.

"Who will get the big chair?"
said Chicken Little.

"Who will get
the little chair?" said Chicken Big.

"Let us play a game," they said
"One, two, three, GO!"

Chicken Big chased Chicken Little across the room.

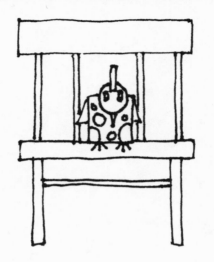

Chicken Little sat in the
big chair.

Chicken Big cheered and clapped her wings.

Chicken Little got up. She chased Chicken Big.

Chicken Big sat in the
little chair.

Chicken Little cheered and clapped her wings.

But all of a sudden , the little
chair creaked, croaked, and BROKE!

Chicken Big crashed to the ground.

Chicken Little ran to her friend.
"O.K., Chicken Big?" she said.

Chicken Big checked her wings.
She checked her legs.
She nodded her head.

"O.K., Chicken Little", she bravely said.

"Then let's play another game,"
said Chicken Little.

"One, two, three, GO!" and off they ran.

Chicken Little ran to the big chair.

Chicken Big ran to the big chair.

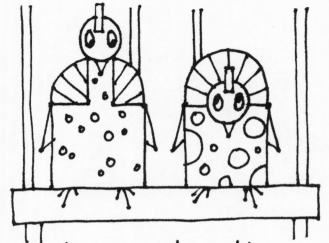

They sat down together, and
as far as I know, they are
sitting there still.

The End

Book 7 adds:

Blend:
ch   -   chicken

Vowel Combinations:
ie   -   friend
ea   -   head